It was also not a place for an elephant.

Not for a giraffe.

Not for a zebra.

Not for a donkey.

Not for a dog.

Not for a cat, a dwarf bunny,

or even a guinea pig.

Papa was allergic to animal hair.

The only thing left was...

A FISH!

Mama didn't seem to be against the idea at first.

Then suddenly she said, "I'm afraid you might be too young."

Too young?

Me?

For a fish?

That night I sat looking out the window.

The rain was beating against the glass.

Could it be that heaven was as sad as I was?

I cried myself to sleep while it rained and rained.

It rained for hours.

It rained for days.

The water in the river kept rising.

First it flooded the street that ran along the river.

Then the water reached our building.

We could only get to town with a boat.

That was something I couldn't have imagined in my wildest dreams.

It was like being in a gondola in Venice.

Everything was so still.

Suddenly, I saw something that gave me a start.

"Stop!" I shouted.

In the lavender bush next to the fountain something shiny was wildly
flip-flopping around. Was it a dragon?

Was it a crocodile?   No, it was...

A FISH!

I grabbed the bucket, pushed it into the water and shook the lavender bush to free the poor fish.

Two seconds later he was in the boat with me.

"It doesn't get any fresher than that," Papa said, "now what?"

"Quick, let's get home." I said.

I was able to bring my mom the freshest fish she'd ever seen.

But it didn't end up in the frying pan.

No, it ended up in the bathtub.

That's right!

Fresh – I just had to name him that – wasn't small.

He wasn't colorful either.

But he was a fish, my fish.

I was very happy.

A week later the river shrank
back to where it belonged.
Fresh was still in the bathtub.
"You know," my mother said, "we can't
keep bathing at the neighbors forever."
I wasn't worried a bit about the neighbors or the tub. I was only worried
about one thing.
Fresh didn't look happy. Every day he got paler and quieter. I took good
care of him. I fed him regularly and made a really comfy home for him.
But it didn't help at all.

Finally, one evening I said to him, "You don't want to be here, do you?
You want to be free in the big river."
Fresh didn't say a word, but a little air bubble popped up.
His wish was clear.
The tub was much too small and smooth, not like a river at all.
I sighed. Should I or shouldn't I?
That night I didn't sleep a wink.

By the next morning I had made up my mind.

Even before my parents were awake,
I went to the old bridge with Fresh.

"So long, Fresh,
my friend," I whispered.
He was very still as I gave him
a kiss on his slippery nose.
When I let him go, he sprang high in
a big arc and then back into his river.
Colorful drops of water sprayed up like
little rainbows in the morning sun.

Then he disappeared in the river forever.

On the way home I stopped and emptied the bucket over the lavender bush.
Standing by the fountain, I cried so hard I thought I would cause the next flood.

As soon as my mother saw me she knew what I had done.
She hugged me.
"I knew you would let him go," she said softly. "You loved him a lot. Now come with me."

She took me by the hand and led me to the bathroom.

There, sitting on the little table by the bathtub, was a round fishbowl.
In the clear water a frisky little fish swam wildly back and forth.
It was tiny and so colorful, just like a rainbow.
I decided to call him Frisky.
"I know now that you can take care of a fish," said my mother.
"And for your birthday your father is going to build you a real
aquarium so the little fish won't have to be alone."

I jumped up and hugged my mother.